Lots and Lots of Chicken Pox

Written by Jane Carroll
Illustrated by Virginia Barrett

An easy-to-read SOLO
for beginning readers

Scholastic Canada Ltd.
Toronto New York London Auckland Sydney
Mexico City New Delhi Hong Kong Buenos Aires

Scholastic Canada Ltd.
175 Hillmount Road, Markham, Ontario, Canada L6C 1Z7

Scholastic Inc.
555 Broadway, New York, NY 10012, USA

Scholastic Australia Pty Limited
PO Box 579, Gosford, NSW 2250, Australia

Scholastic New Zealand Limited
Private Bag 94407, Greenmount, Auckland, New Zealand

Scholastic Ltd.
Villiers House, Clarendon Avenue, Leamington Spa,
Warwickshire CV32 5PR, UK

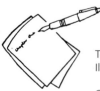

First published by Omnibus Books, part of the
SCHOLASTIC GROUP, Sydney, Australia.

National Library of Canada Cataloguing in Publication
Carroll, Jane
    Lots and lots of chicken pox / written by Jane Carroll;
illustrated by Virginia Barrett.
(Solo reading)
First published in Australia under title: Jade McKade.
ISBN 0-7791-1393-4
    I. Barrett, Virginia II. Title. III. Series.
PZ7.C248Lo 2002   j823   C2002-902097-2

5 4 3 2 1   Printed and bound in Canada   02 03 04 05

For Jeanie, who didn't want to
go to school – J.C.

For Katy – V.B.

Chapter 1

Jade McKade loved to climb the tree in her backyard. She loved to race her go-cart down the hill.

She loved to play monsters and dragons with the kids next door.

But Jade McKade didn't love going to school.

Every morning at breakfast time she said, "I don't want to go to school."

All the way to the bus stop she shouted, "I don't want to go to school!"

In the bus she wrote with her finger on the window, *I don't want to go to school.*

Chapter 2

One morning Jade wouldn't get out of bed.

"It's time you got dressed," said Mum.

"You'll be late for school," said Dad.

"And you'll make me late, too!" yelled Jemma, her big sister.

"Buzz off, you big blowflies!"
said Jade from under the covers.

Jade took so long to get out of bed, she and Jemma missed the bus. Mum said, "I'll have to drive you. I'll be late for work. Get into the car. Hurry up!"

"But I haven't had breakfast!" said Jade.

"Bring it with you," said Mum.

"But I'm still in my pyjamas!"
wailed Jade.

"Then you can go to school in
your pyjamas!" said Mum. "Jade
McKade, we are going to school,
and we are going *now*."

Jade had to get dressed in the car. All the way she shouted, "I don't want to go to school! I don't want to go to school!"

Mum took Jade and Jemma into the playground. The other kids were lining up to go in to class.

"You're late," said Mum. "Hurry up. Off you go."

Chapter 3

At lunchtime a man came with a camera to take the children's photos.

The boys and girls in Jade's class did their hair. They brushed the crumbs off their sweaters.

They lined up in rows with
the tallest at the back and the
smallest at the front. They held
their hands behind their backs.

"Big smile!" said the man with the camera.

Jade frowned.

"We'll try that again," said the man. "All together, say *cheese*."

"Cheeeeeeese!" said the children.

"Rats," said Jade, and folded her arms.

"Little girl in the front row," said the man, "you're spoiling the photo."

"Jade McKade, where's your happy smile?" said the teacher.

"Jade McKade, you're terrible," whispered her friend, Gabby Green. She smiled at Jade and Jade smiled back.

Chapter 4

The next morning Mum said,
"Time to get up, Jade."

Dad said, "Hurry up and get
dressed, Jade."

Jemma said, "If you make me
late for school today, I'll turn you
into a bug and stomp on you!"

Jade pulled the covers up to her chin and said, "I feel sick."

"Don't be silly," said Mum.
"Don't pretend," said Dad.
"Do you want me to stomp on you now?" yelled Jemma.

"But I've got spots," wailed Jade. "I *am* sick."

And she was.

Chapter 5

Jade had spots on her face and spots on her tummy. She had spots in her ears and spots in her throat.

She had spots between her toes and spots up her nose.

She wasn't allowed to go to school. She had to stay home in bed.

That afternoon Jemma came
home from school and counted
the spots on Jade's tummy.

"Four hundred and six,"
she said. "Today Gabby Green
brought a birthday cake to school.
She kept a piece and asked me to
bring it home for you. But I knew
you were sick, so I ate it."

"See if I care," said Jade.

Chapter 6

The next afternoon Jemma counted the spots on Jade's back. "Three hundred and seventy-seven," she said. "Today was Games Day. We had sack races and egg-and-spoon races. We had a Jumping Castle too."

"So what?" said Jade.

The next afternoon Jemma
counted the spots between Jade's
toes.

"Sixty-three," she said.
"Tomorrow all the kids from
school are going to the fair."

"Can I come too?" said Jade.
"You have to stay in bed," said
Jemma. "You're not allowed to go."

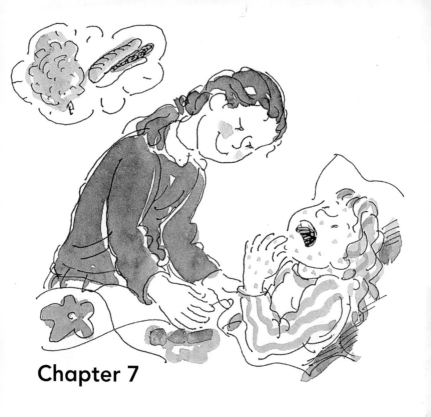

Chapter 7

The next afternoon Jemma
checked the spots in Jade's throat
and the spots in her ears.

She said, "The fair was so much
fun. I had a hot dog and chips
and cotton candy."

"Then I went on the swings and I wasn't even sick. Gabby Green said she wished you were there."

Jade didn't say anything. A big tear sneaked down her cheek.

That night, when Mum came to kiss her goodnight, Jade said, "Mum, when can I go back to school?"

"As soon as the spots are gone
and you feel better," said Mum.
She looked at Jade's tummy.
"Lots of spots have gone already.
You'll be better soon." She gave
Jade a hug and kissed her
goodnight.

Chapter 8

When the spots were all gone and Jade felt better, Mum drove her to school.

Jade and Jemma walked in to the playground together. The kids in Jade's class ran up to say hello.

Gabby Green said, "You can sit next to me at lunchtime." Then she said, "Guess what? We're having a fairy tale costume parade. I'm the princess."

"What am I?" said Jade.

"You're the dragon," said Gabby.

"That's good," said Jade. "I like being a dragon."

Chapter 9

All the mums and dads came to see the parade. They clapped and cheered.

Jade's mum and dad clapped the loudest for the dragon.

After the parade the teacher
took a photo of the children in
their costumes. "Look this way,"
he said. "Say *cheese!*"

"*Cheeeeeeeese!*" said the king, the queen, the princess, the witch and all the elves and fairies.

47

"Rats," said the dragon, and giggled.

Jane Carroll

When my mum was a little girl she didn't want to go to school. She walked along the brick wall outside her house singing, "I don't want to go to school, I don't want to go to school."

One day she got very sick. She had to stay home in bed for weeks. After a while she got bored with being at home. She wanted to go back to school! She kept singing, "I *want* to go to school, I *want* to go to school."

When my mum told me this I laughed. That's why I wrote the story about Jade McKade.

Virginia Barrett

Before I could draw the pictures for this book, I needed a model. I had to find a little girl who looked the way I thought Jade McKade did. I knew someone named Tina who had four daughters. If none of them was right, maybe Tina knew other little girls I could draw. I went to see her. The door was opened by my perfect Jade! There she was, with her hair all over the place, wearing jeans, and with a wicked smile. How lucky!

Thanks Katy, and thanks Tina!